There are many versions of this classic tale. In the tradition of the storyteller, each one is uniquely different.

Library of Congress Cataloging-in-Publication Data

José, Eduard.
  Fearless John.

  (A Classic tale)
  Translation of: Juan sin miedo.
  Summary: Fearless John survives encounters
with a ghost and three giants and wins the right to
ask the king's daughter for her hand in marriage.
  [1. Fairy tales.   2. Folklore]   I. Lavarello,
José M., ill.   II. Moncure, Jane Belk.
III. Fearless John.   IV. Title.   V. Series.
PZ8.J747Fe 1988   398.2'1   [E]   88-35215
ISBN 0-89565-470-9

© 1988 Parramón Ediciones, S. A.
Printed in Spain by Sirven Gráfic, S. A.
© Alexander Publishers' Marketing
and The Child's World, Inc.: English
edition, 1988.
L.D.: B-44.036-88

A CLASSIC TALE

Fearless John

Illustration: José M. Lavarello
Adaptation: Eduard José

Retold by Jane Belk Moncure

The Child's World, Inc.

Once upon a time, in a village far away, there lived a boy who was not afraid of anything. This boy, named John, was never afraid because he didn't know what fear was.

"What does fear look like?" he asked his father one day. "Is fear big or small? Is fear round or square? Is it light, like smoke? Or heavy, like a stone?"

"You will find out someday," said his father. "Someday you will feel fear all the way down to your toes."

"Will it tickle?" asked John.

"Wait and see," said his father.

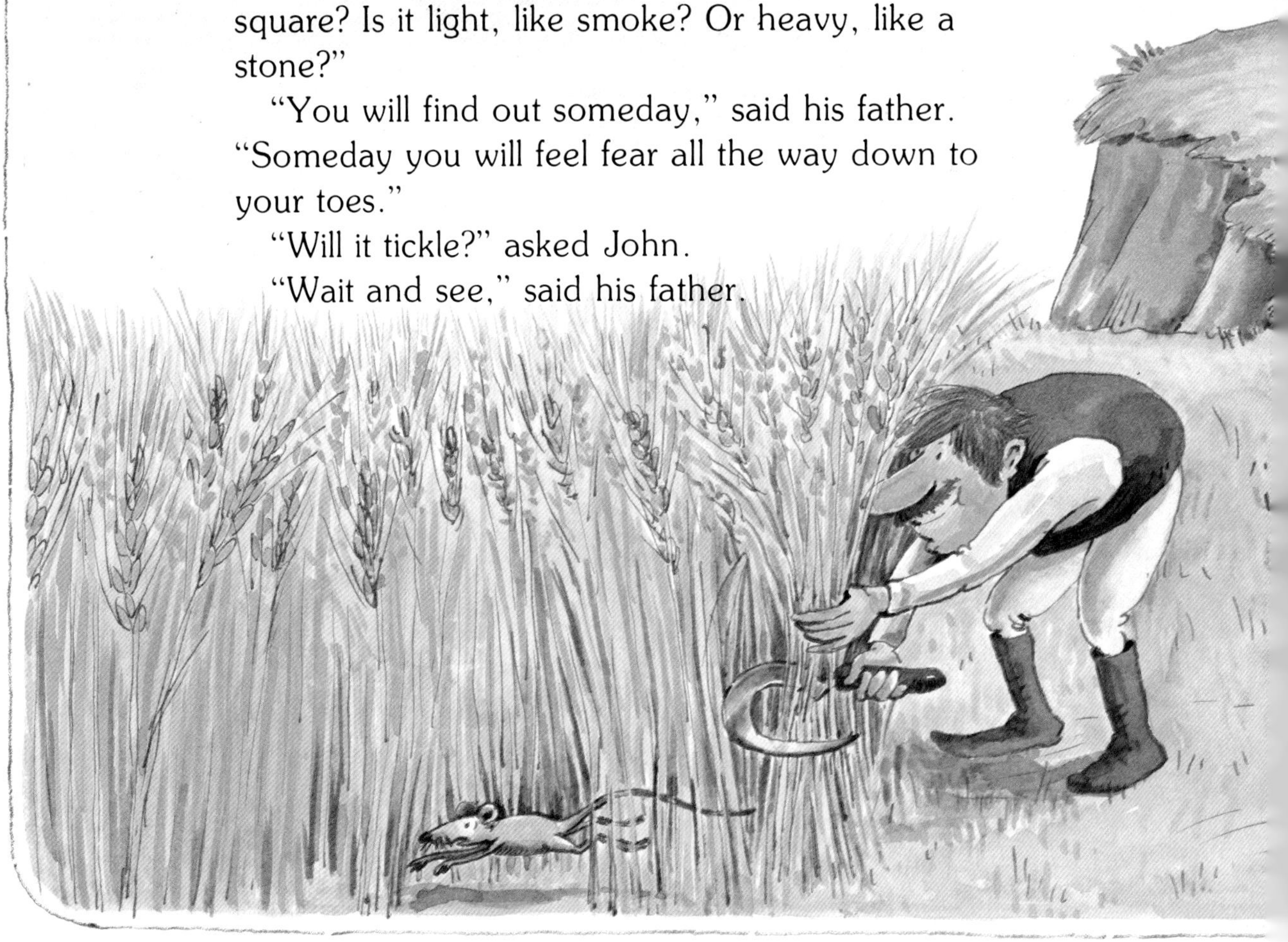

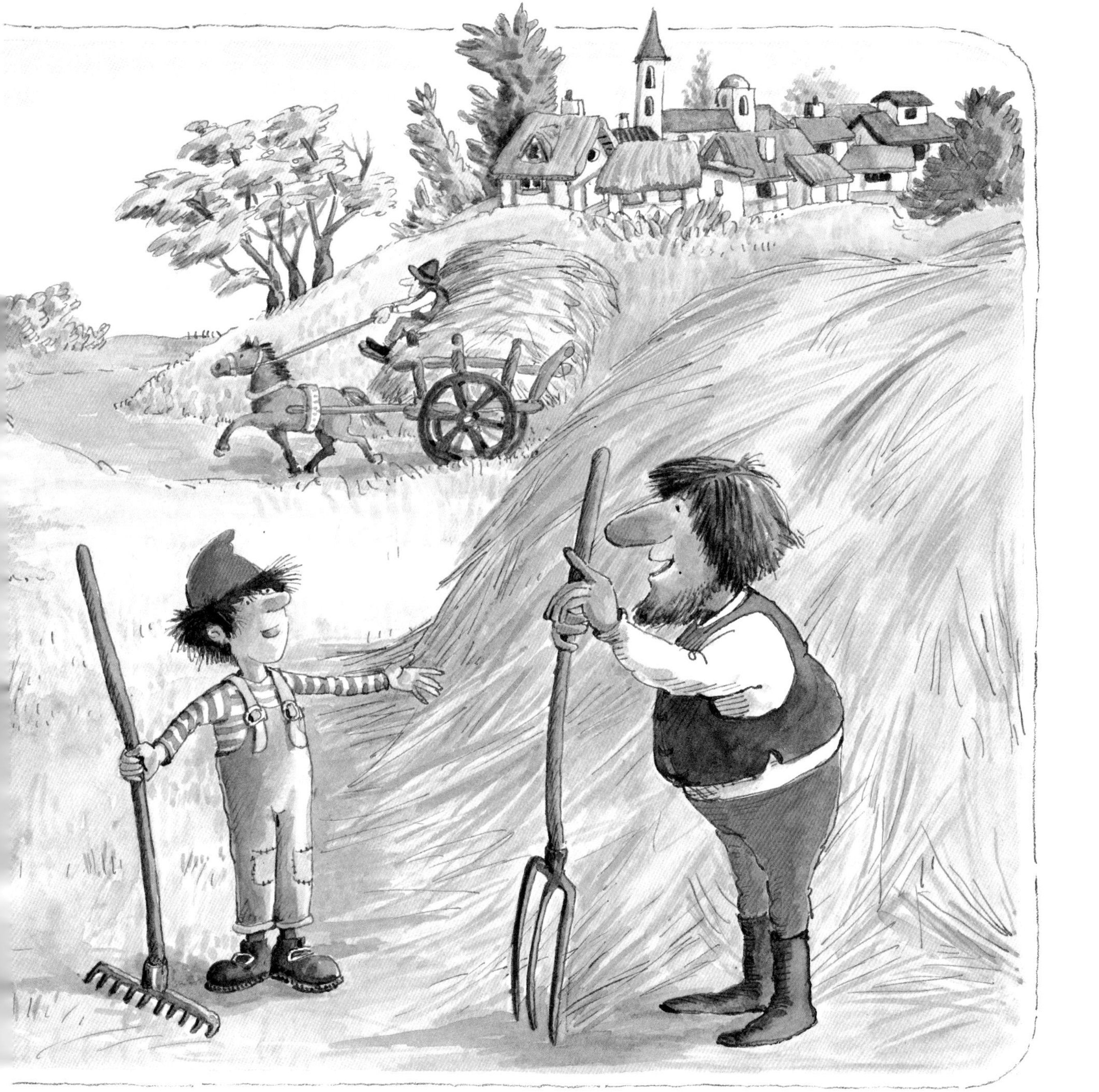

But John could not wait. "I will go and find fear for myself, even if I have to travel around the world," he said. So off he went, whistling a merry tune. Soon it began to get dark, and John decided to find a place to sleep. He stopped at an old inn.

"There is no room here," said the innkeeper. "But if you dare, you can go to the big old house on the other side of the village. It is deserted."

"If I dare?" asked John. "What do you mean by that?"

"Well, they say the house is full of ghosts. Nobody dares to go near it. They are all afraid."

"Afraid? Wonderful! That's what I am searching for!" John clapped his hands for joy.

The innkeeper watched the boy skip merrily toward the haunted house. "That boy is crazy!" the innkeeper said to himself.

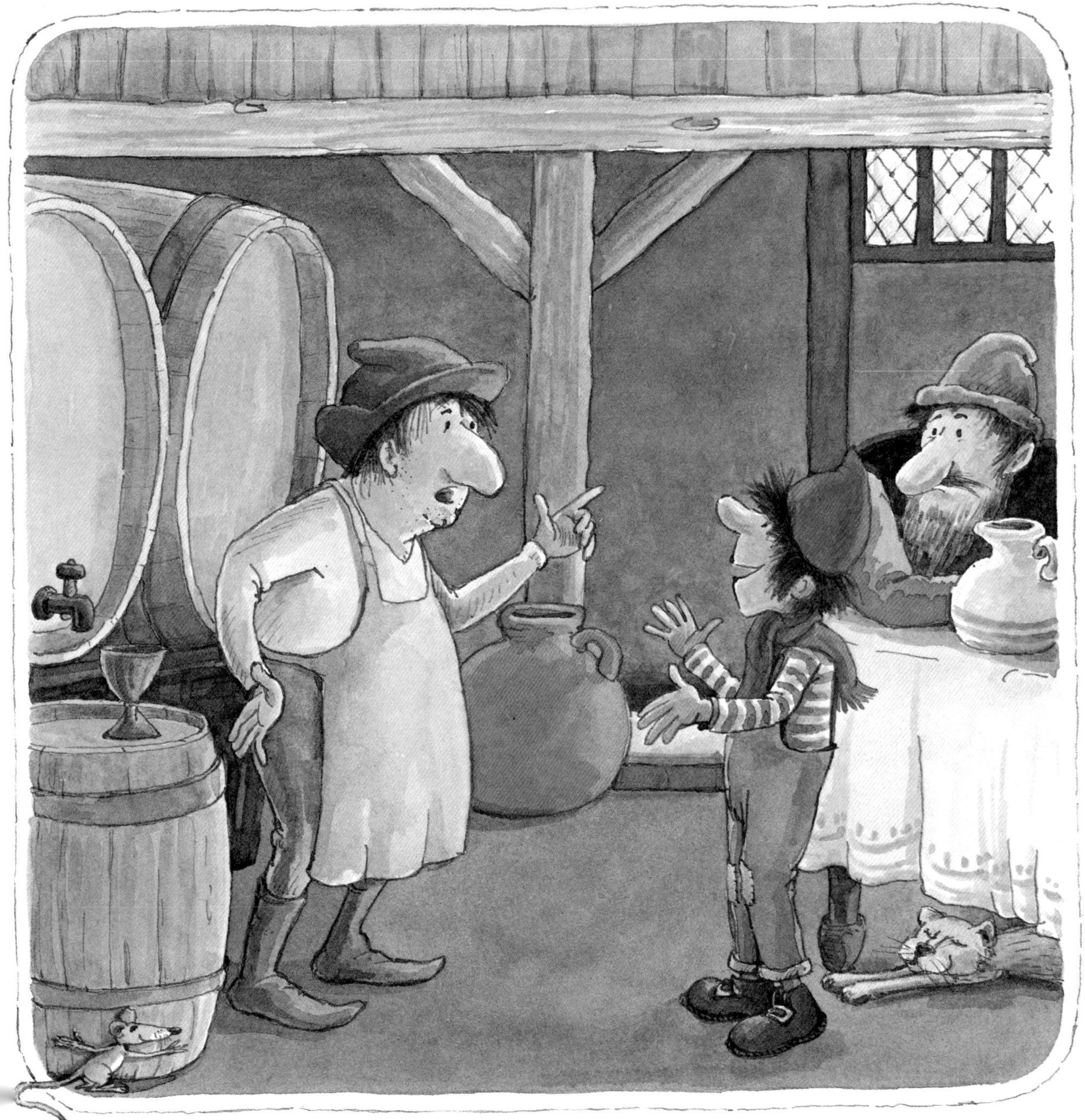

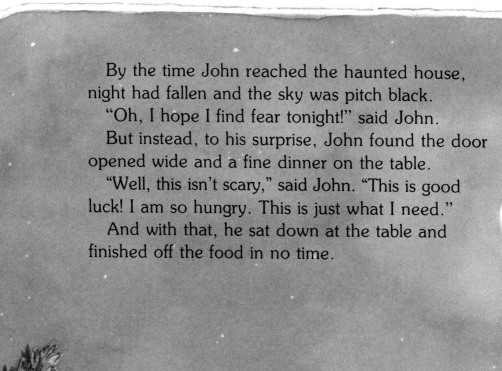

By the time John reached the haunted house,
night had fallen and the sky was pitch black.

"Oh, I hope I find fear tonight!" said John.

But instead, to his surprise, John found the door
opened wide and a fine dinner on the table.

"Well, this isn't scary," said John. "This is good
luck! I am so hungry. This is just what I need."

And with that, he sat down at the table and
finished off the food in no time.

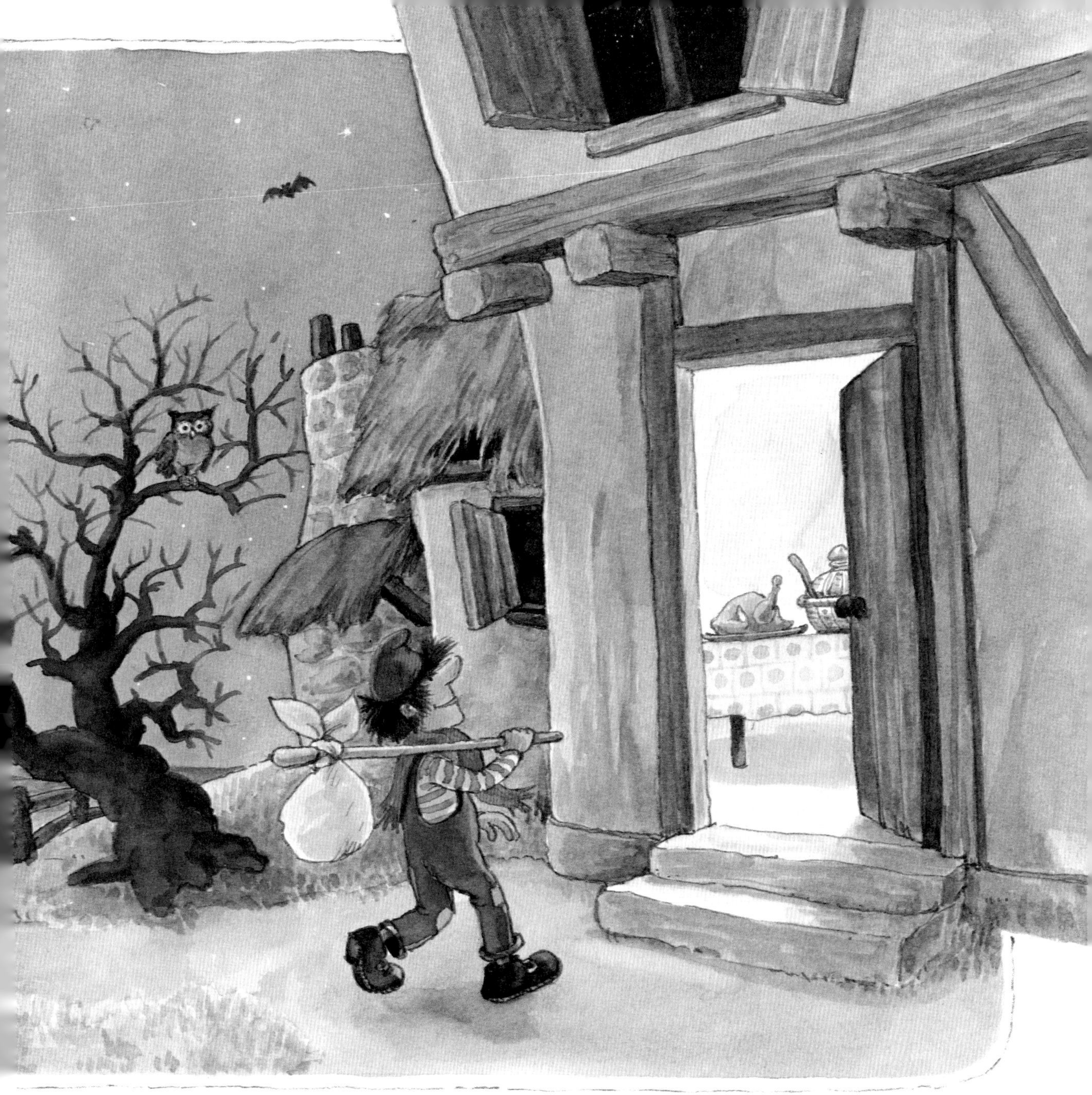

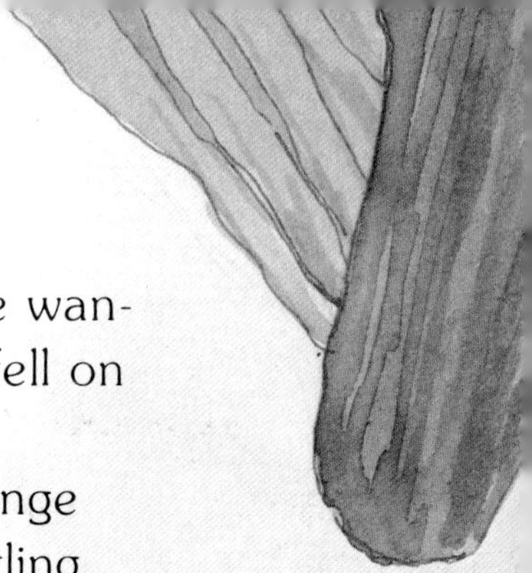

After his big meal, John felt very tired. He wandered upstairs and found a bedroom. John fell on the soft bed and went right to sleep.

But at midnight, he was awakened by strange noises. He heard moans and groans and rattling bones. He heard howls and screams that would have scared even the bravest person. But John did not know what fear was!

He just shouted, "Hey! Be quiet up there! Can't you let me sleep?"

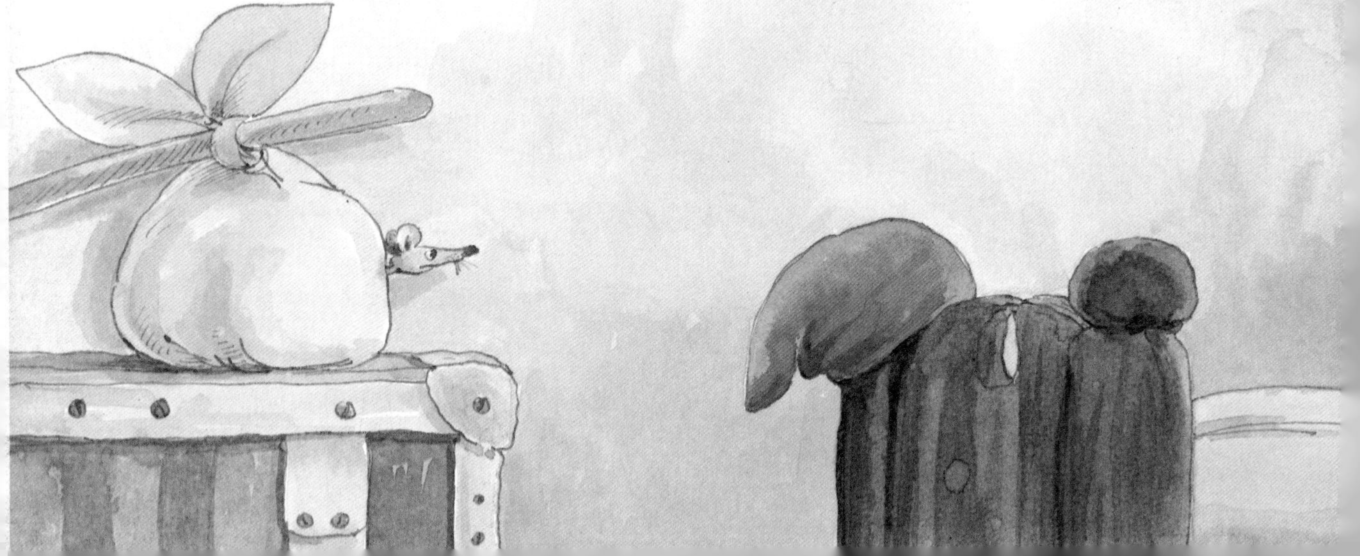

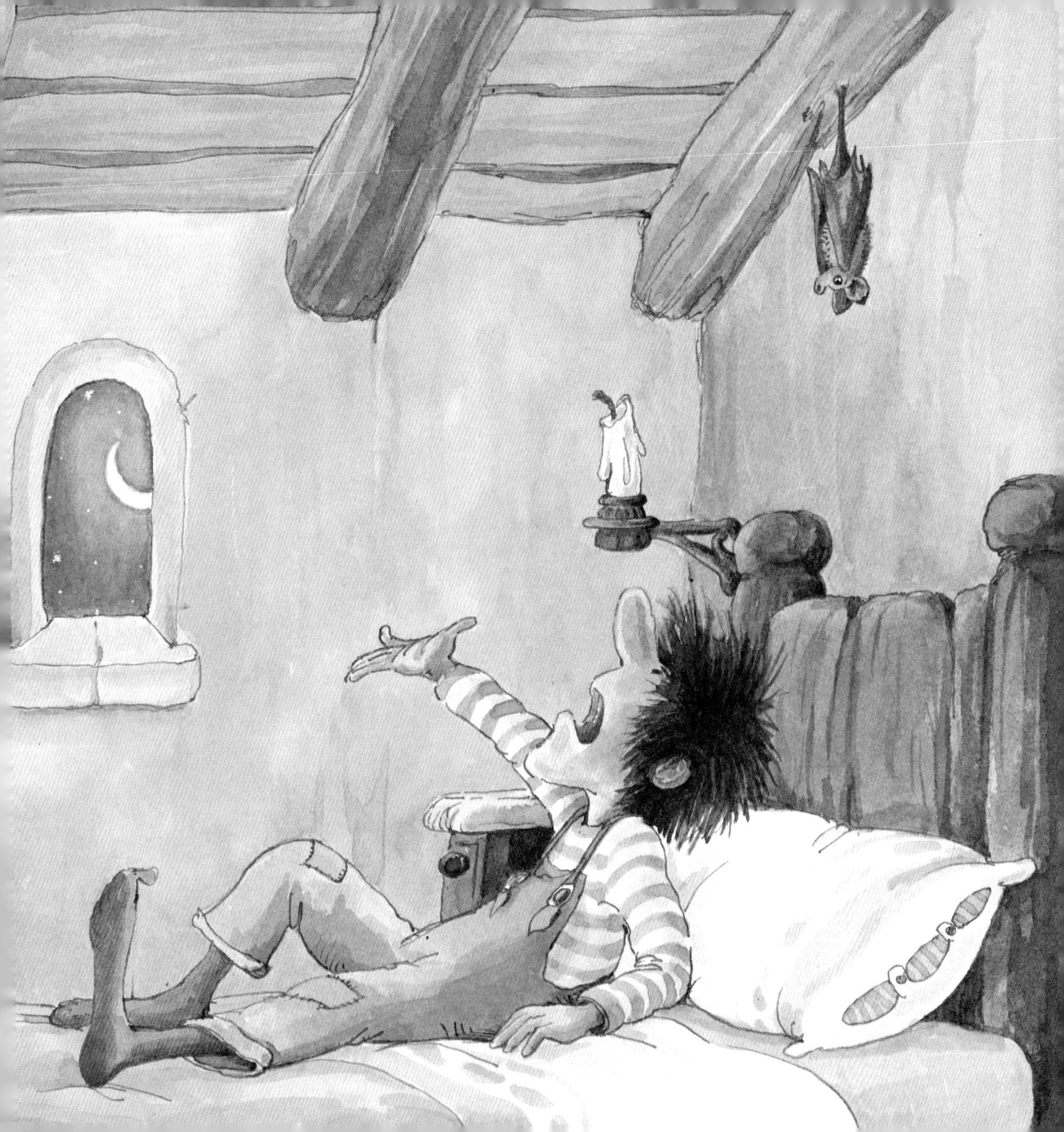

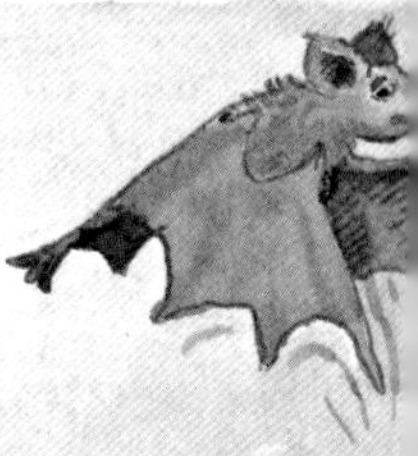

Suddenly, the door opened. In walked a giant ghost. He was holding his head in his arm.

"What's all this shouting about?" asked the giant ghost. "This is my haunted house! You ate my dinner. Now you are sleeping in my bed. Why aren't you afraid of me anyway?"

"I was just wondering," said John. "How does it feel to carry your head like that? I should try it someday."

"So you think it's funny!" roared the ghost. "Well, I'll teach you a lesson!"

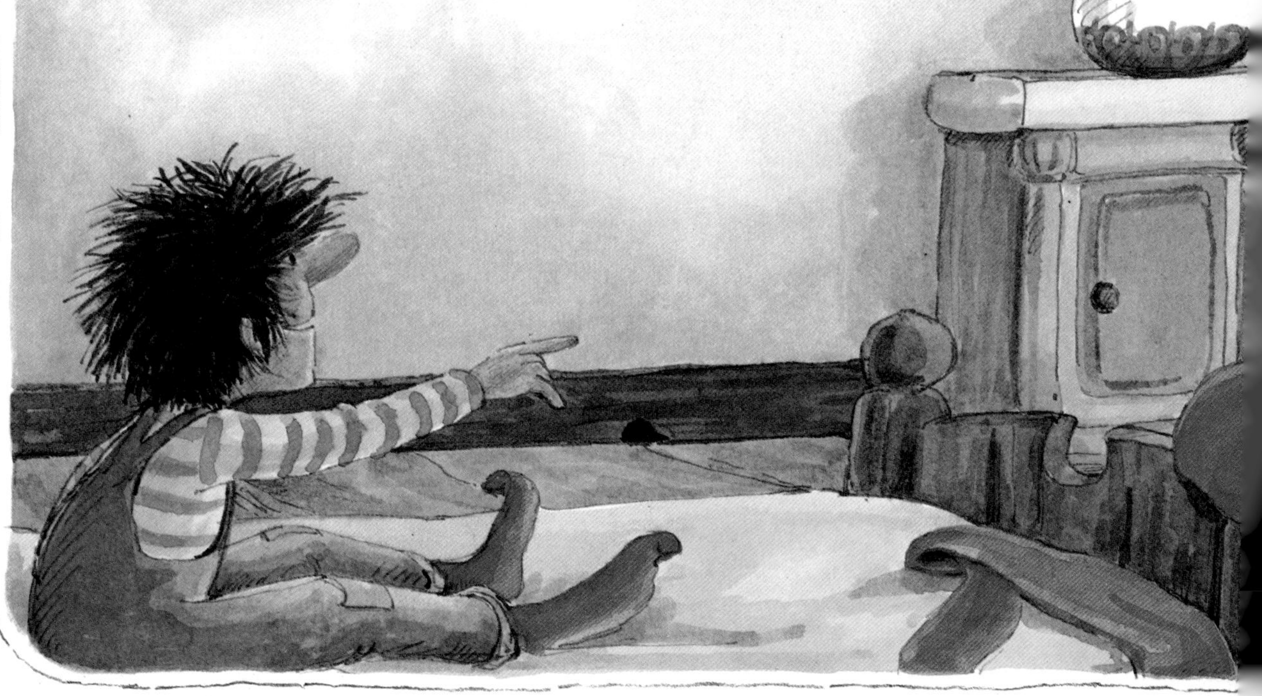

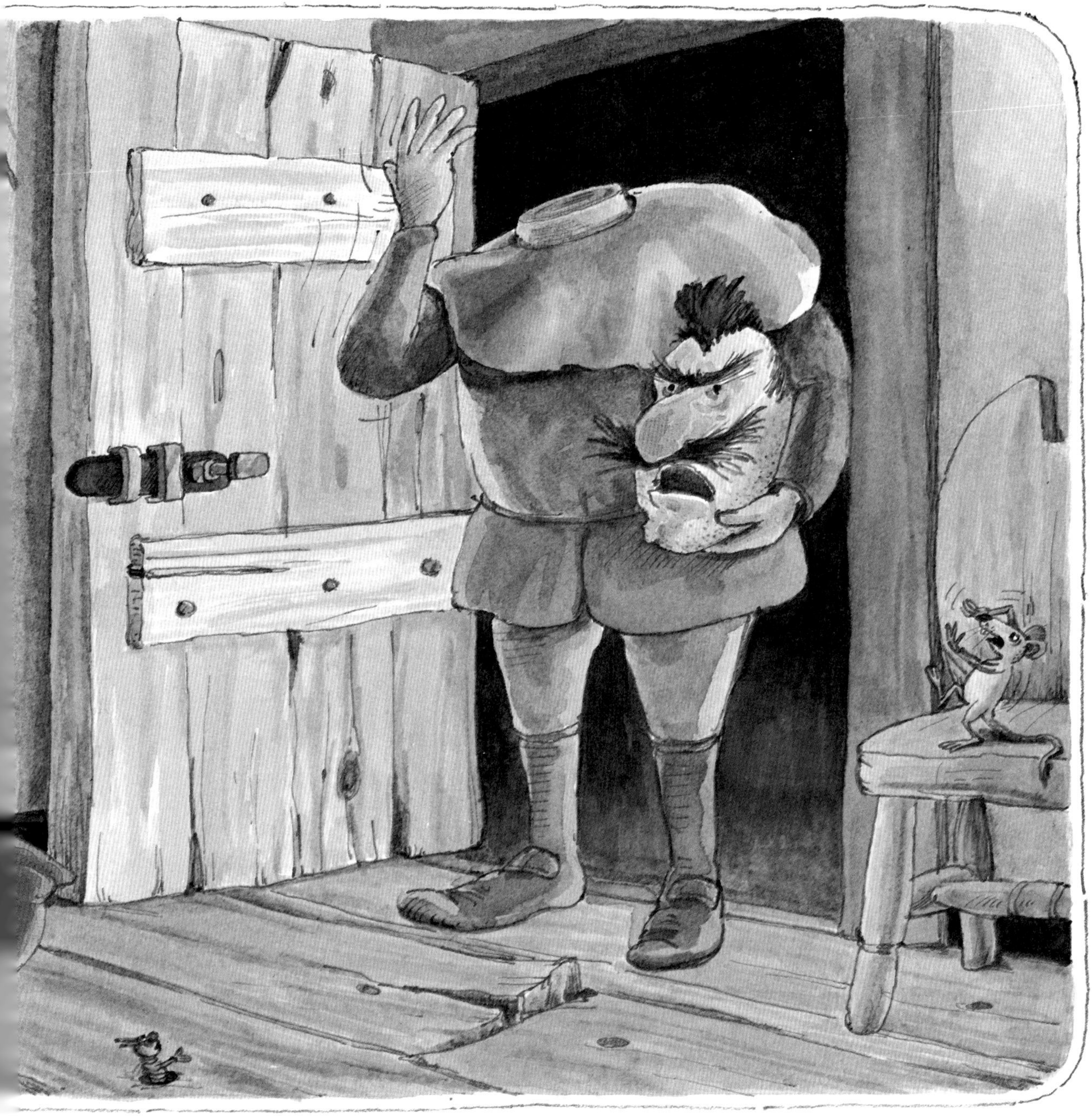

With a wave of his hand, the ghost turned himself into a horrible skeleton that rattled and shook its bones.

"Hey, that's a great trick!" said John. "I like how you dance. Now let's have a pillow fight!" He threw his pillow at the skeleton. When it hit, the bones all fell to pieces and scattered over the floor.

"Great," said John. "Now I have a game."

He lined up the bones like bowling pins. Then he rolled the skeleton's head along the floor and knocked down all the bones.

"Strike!" said John. "Well, this has been fun, but I still haven't found fear. I might as well go back to sleep."

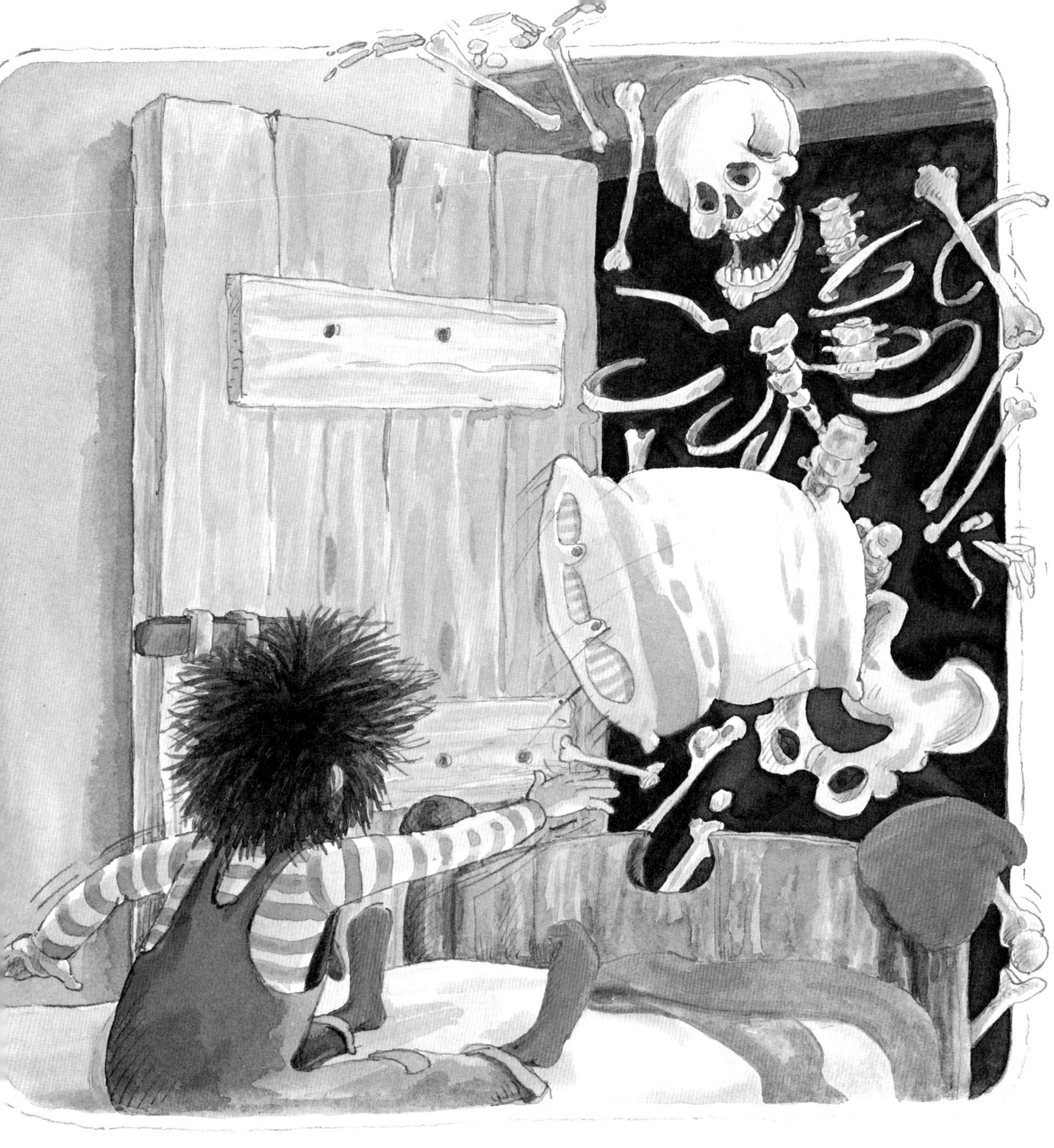

The next morning, the people at the inn asked, "How did you stay in that haunted house all night?"

"Oh! It was nothing," said John. "I slept quite well."

"Were you afraid?" asked the innkeeper.

"Afraid?" asked John. "What is fear?"

But no one could tell him, so he went on his way. After many miles, John became very thirsty. He stopped by a well to have a drink of water. Suddenly, he heard a voice from the bottom of the well.

"You say you do not know what fear is, but if you go to the house on the hill, you will be sure to find it."

"Oh, thank you!" said John. "At last I will find fear."

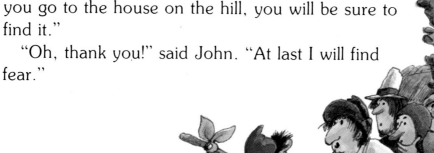

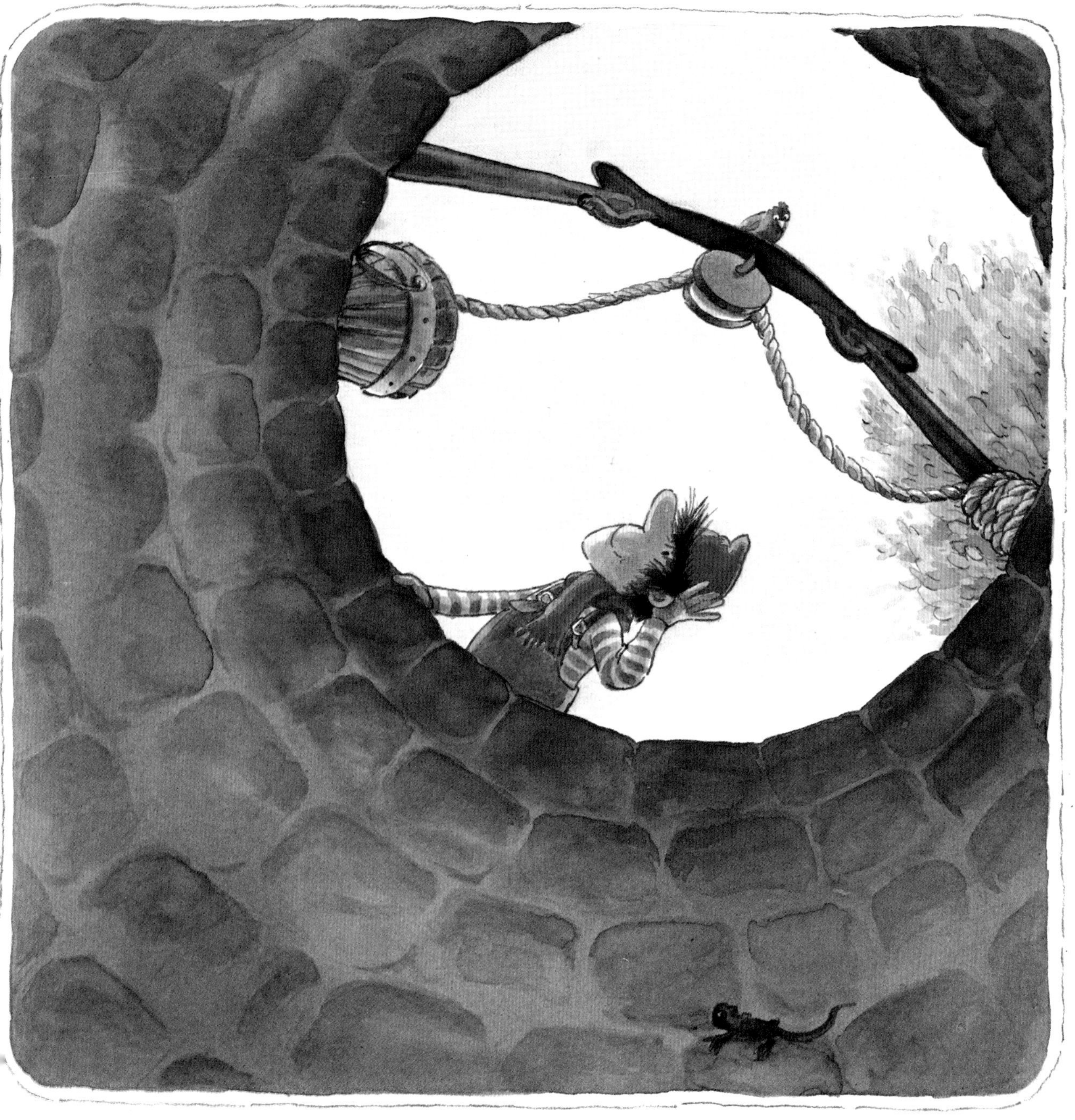

John hurried to the great house on the hill. What a house it was! Everything was so enormous that John knew at once it belonged to giants. But of course he was not afraid, for he did not know what fear was.

He went inside and looked all around, but no one was at home. John was very hungry, so he sat at the giants' table and ate a spoonful of soup, a slice of bread, and a sip of milk.

Once again, John was sleepy after his meal. He went in search of a bed so he could have a nap.

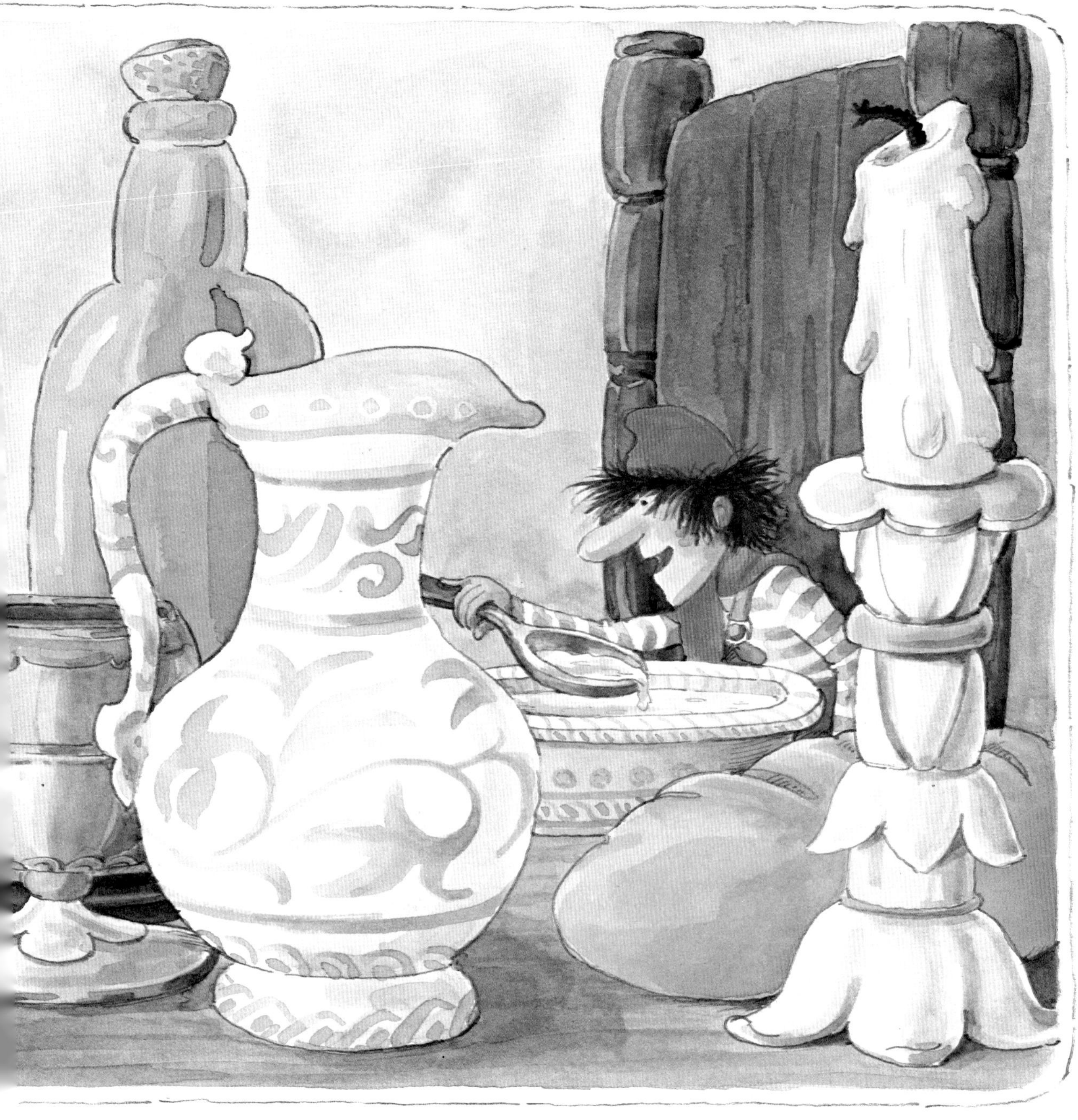

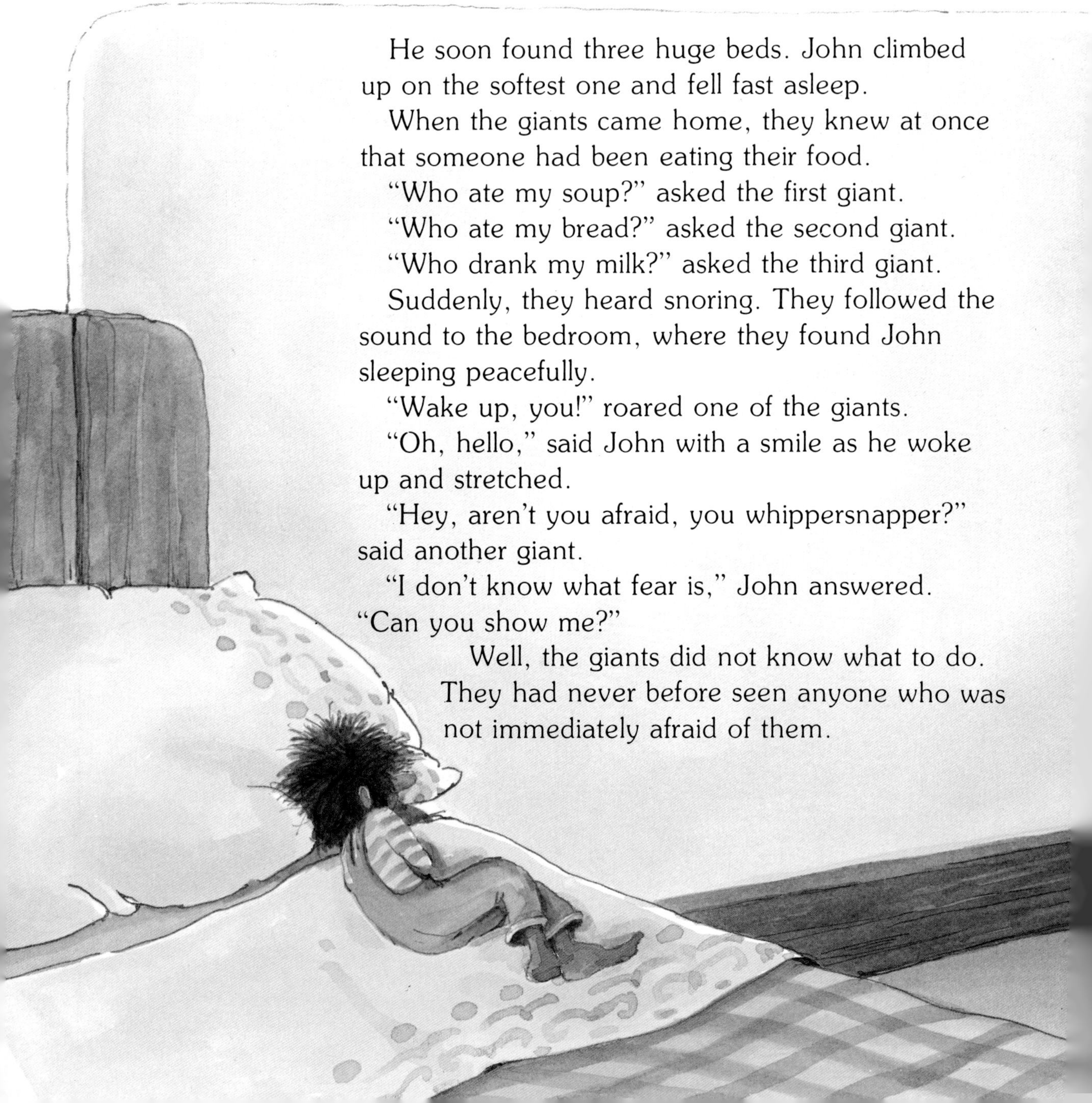

He soon found three huge beds. John climbed up on the softest one and fell fast asleep.

When the giants came home, they knew at once that someone had been eating their food.

"Who ate my soup?" asked the first giant.

"Who ate my bread?" asked the second giant.

"Who drank my milk?" asked the third giant.

Suddenly, they heard snoring. They followed the sound to the bedroom, where they found John sleeping peacefully.

"Wake up, you!" roared one of the giants.

"Oh, hello," said John with a smile as he woke up and stretched.

"Hey, aren't you afraid, you whippersnapper?" said another giant.

"I don't know what fear is," John answered. "Can you show me?"

Well, the giants did not know what to do. They had never before seen anyone who was not immediately afraid of them.

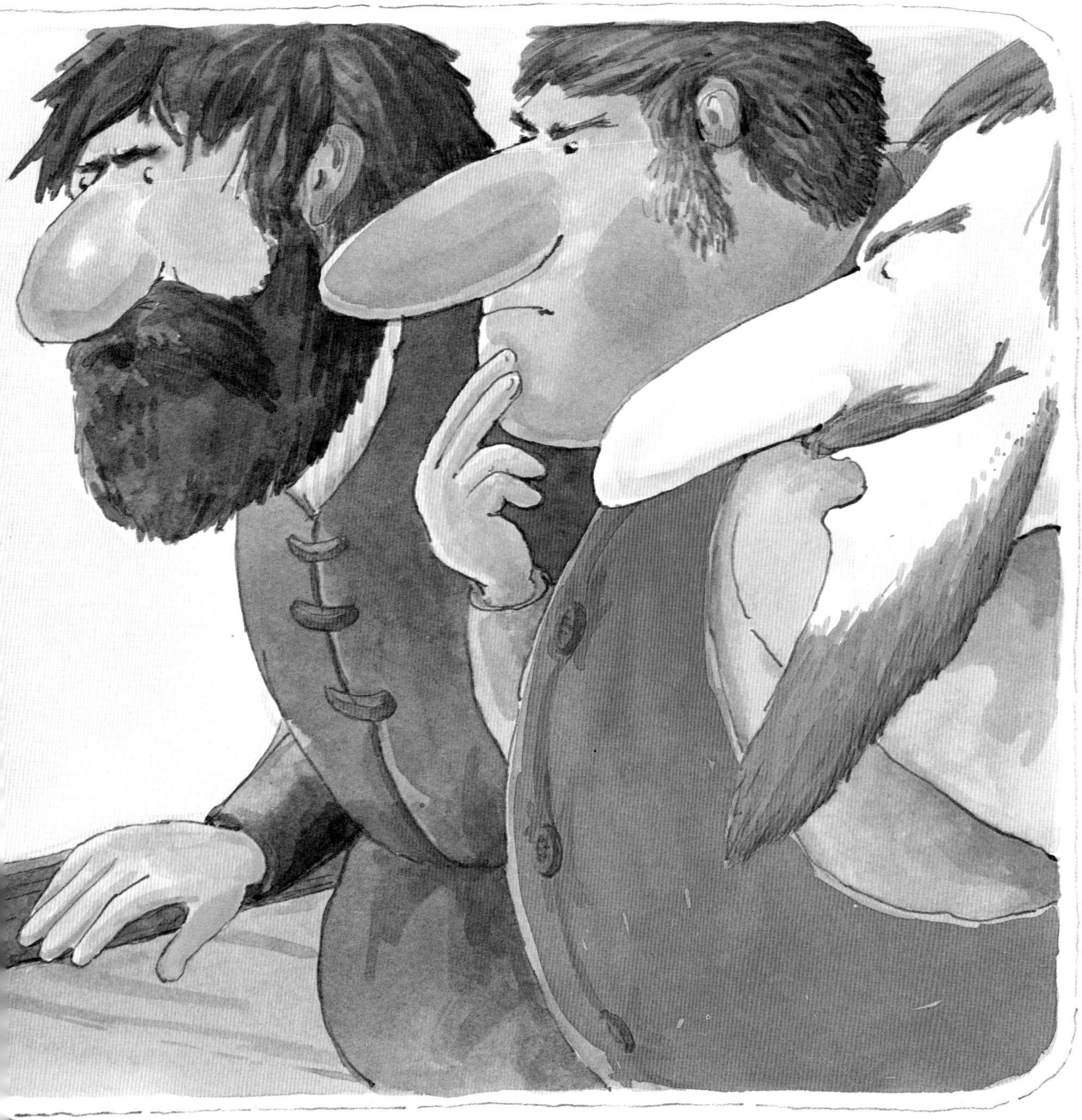

"Please," said John. "All I want is to find out about this fear that everyone talks about!"

The three giants realized that they had found someone braver than they were. So they packed their bags and went far away to find someone to scare.

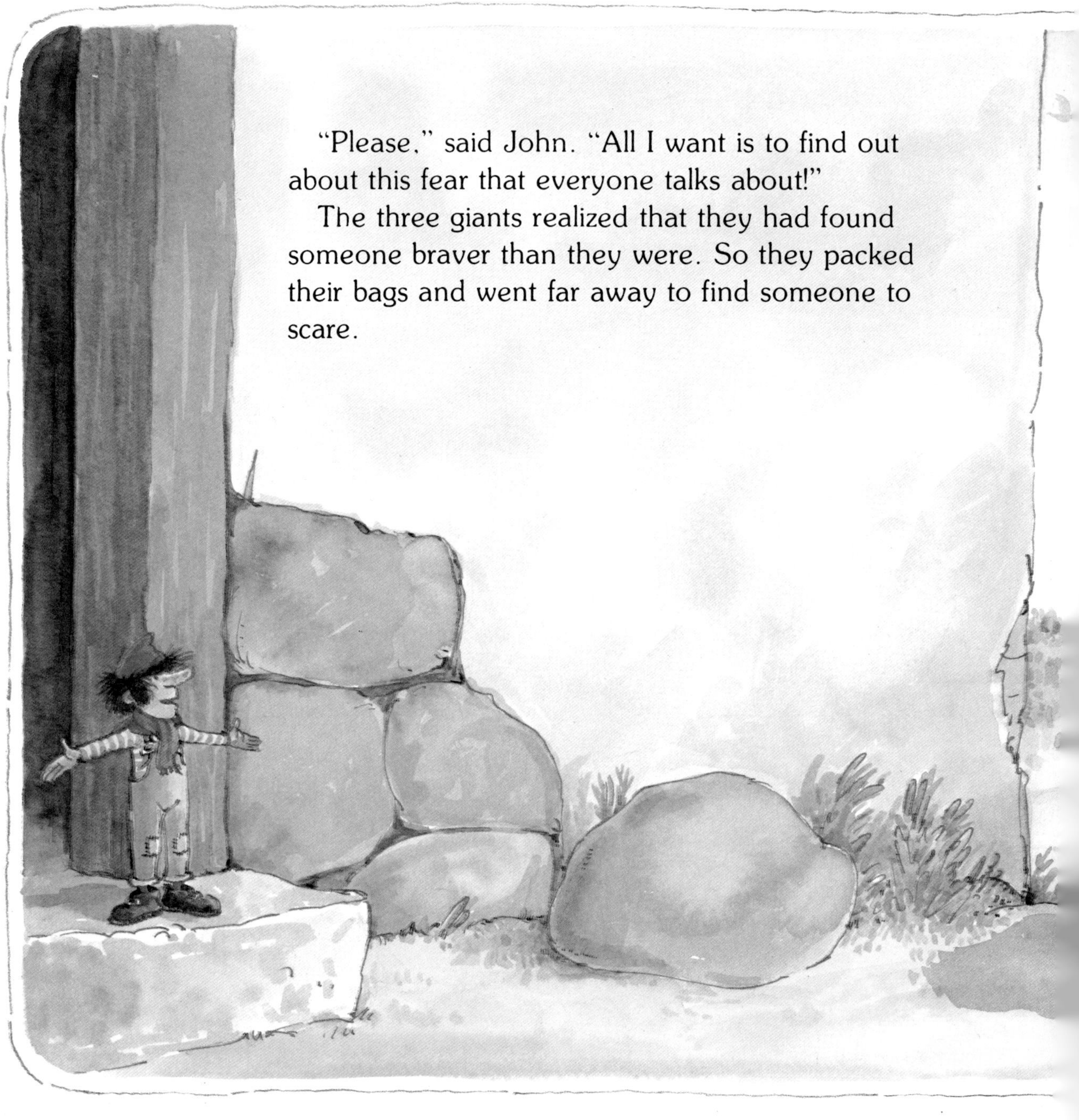

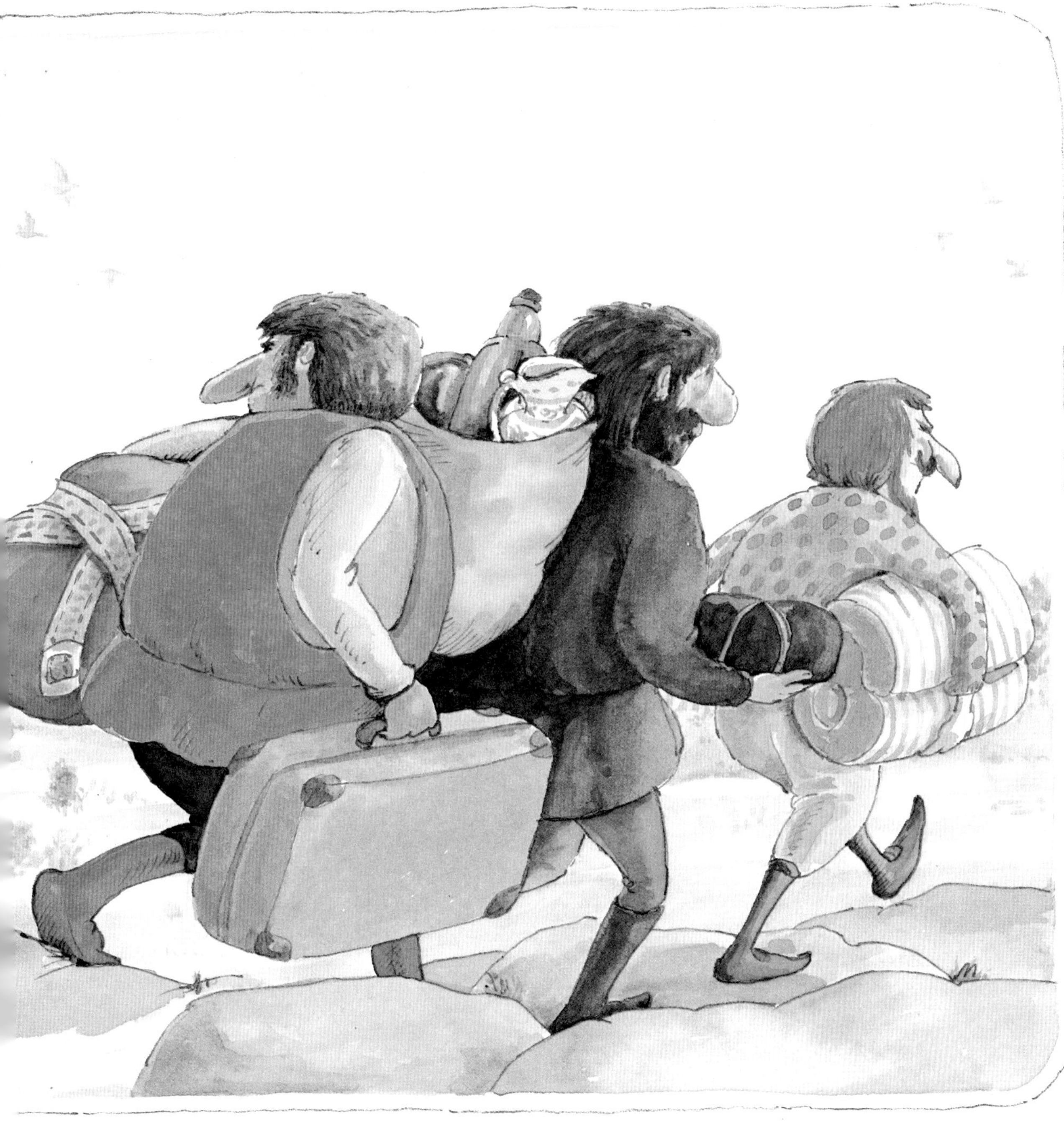

When the king heard about the brave person who had chased away the giants, he asked John to come to the castle.

"You have driven away three terrible giants," he said. "Everyone in the kingdom is grateful to you. Ask anything you wish, and I will give it to you!"

Just then, the king's beautiful daughter passed by. She had heard of John's brave and fearless deed too. When the two young people's eyes met, they fell in love at once.

"I was going to ask you to show me what fear is," said John. "But now that I have seen your daughter, I can only ask you for her hand in marriage. She is the most beautiful girl I have ever seen."

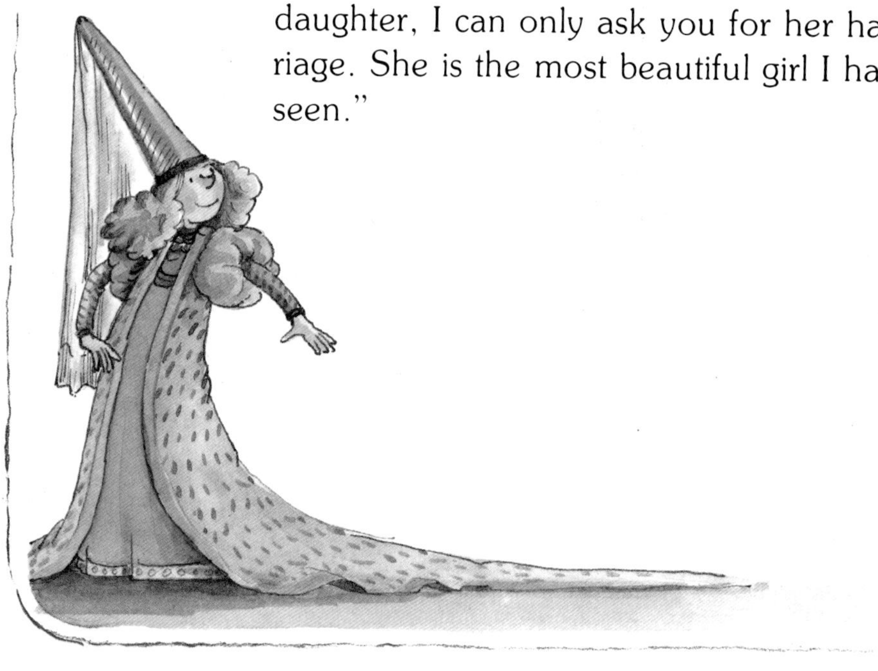

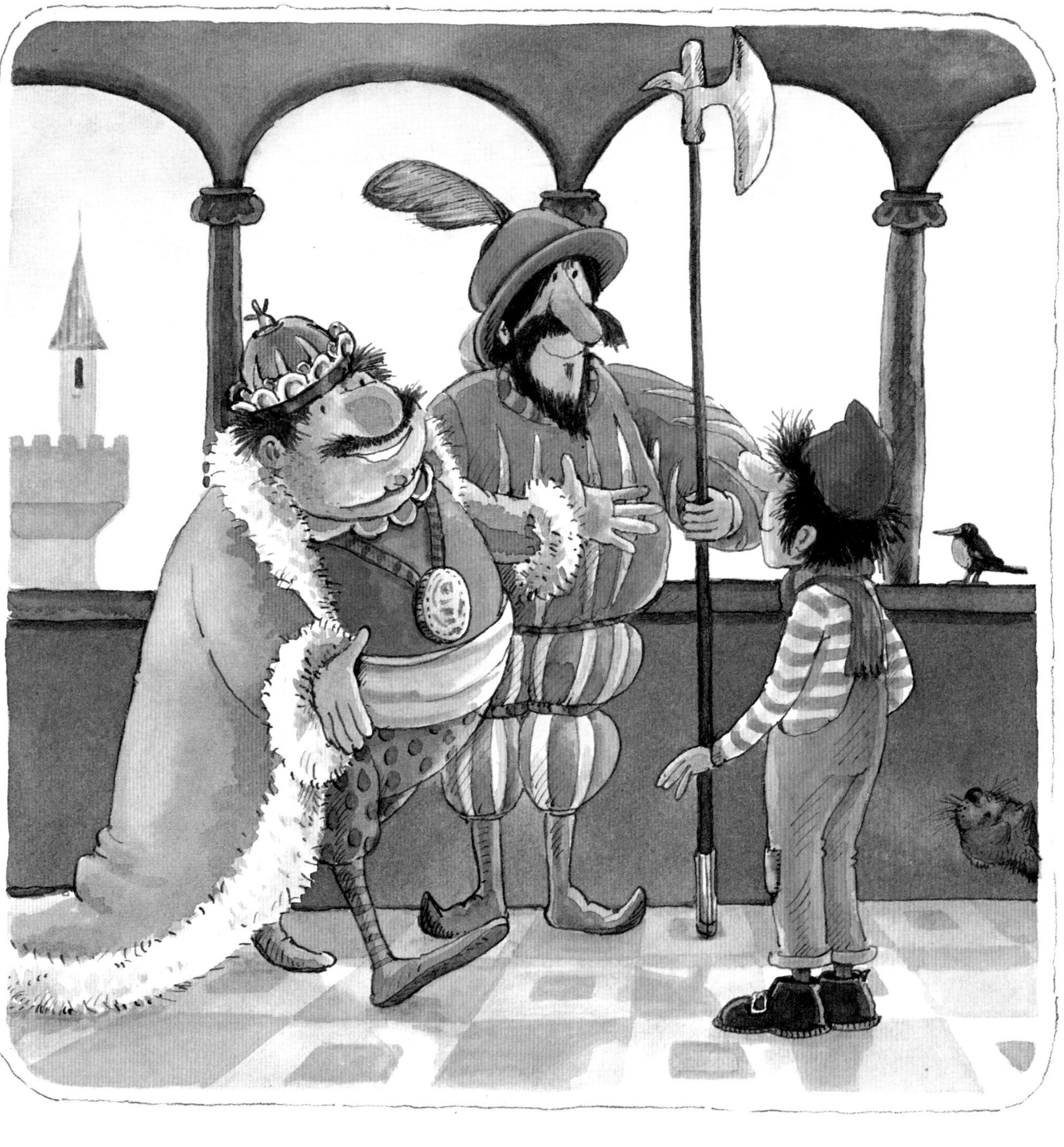

The king was happy that such a brave man should want to marry his daughter, so he said, "You must ask my daughter. If she agrees, you have my blessing."

Though they had fallen in love at first sight, the princess and John spent several months getting to know each other better. Then the princess agreed to marry John.

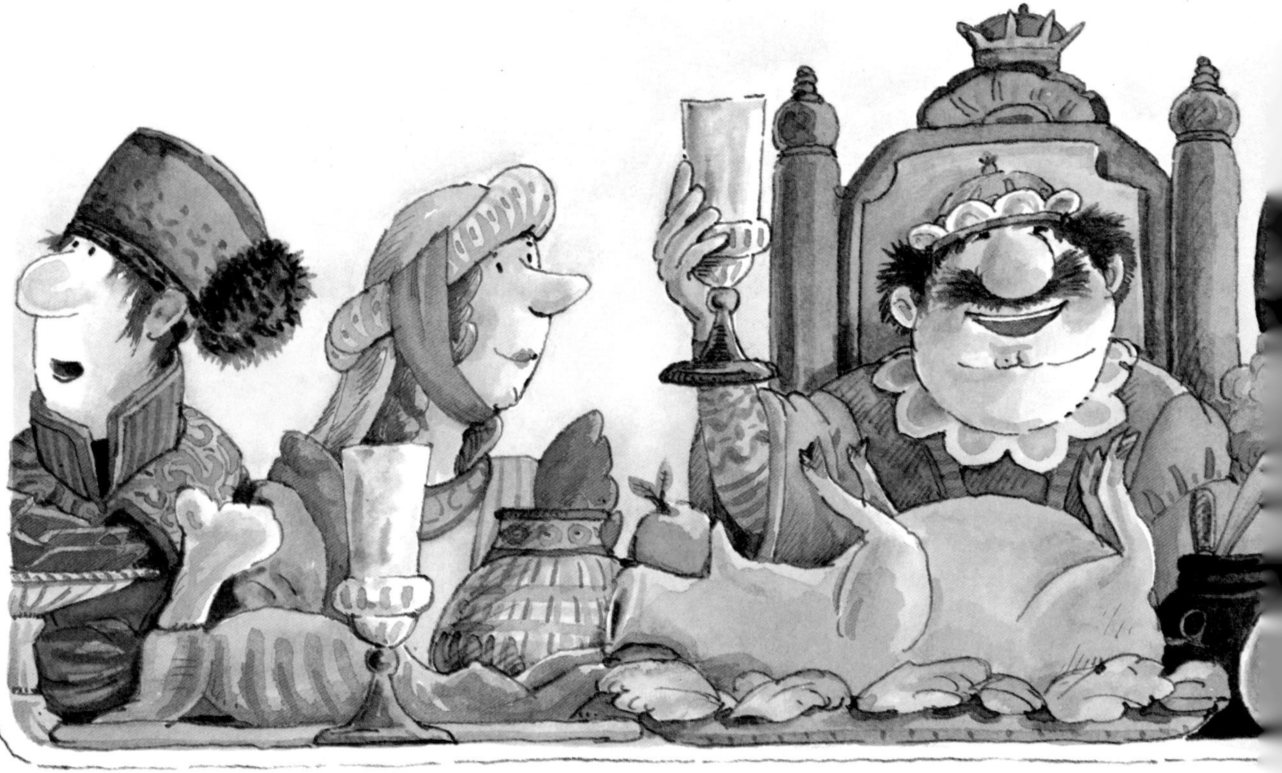

The king had a great celebration in honor of the princess and her new husband, the prince. Everyone in the king's court thought the young prince was the bravest man in all the land.

John was the happiest he had ever been, for he loved his kind wife. But he still had one wish—to know what fear is.

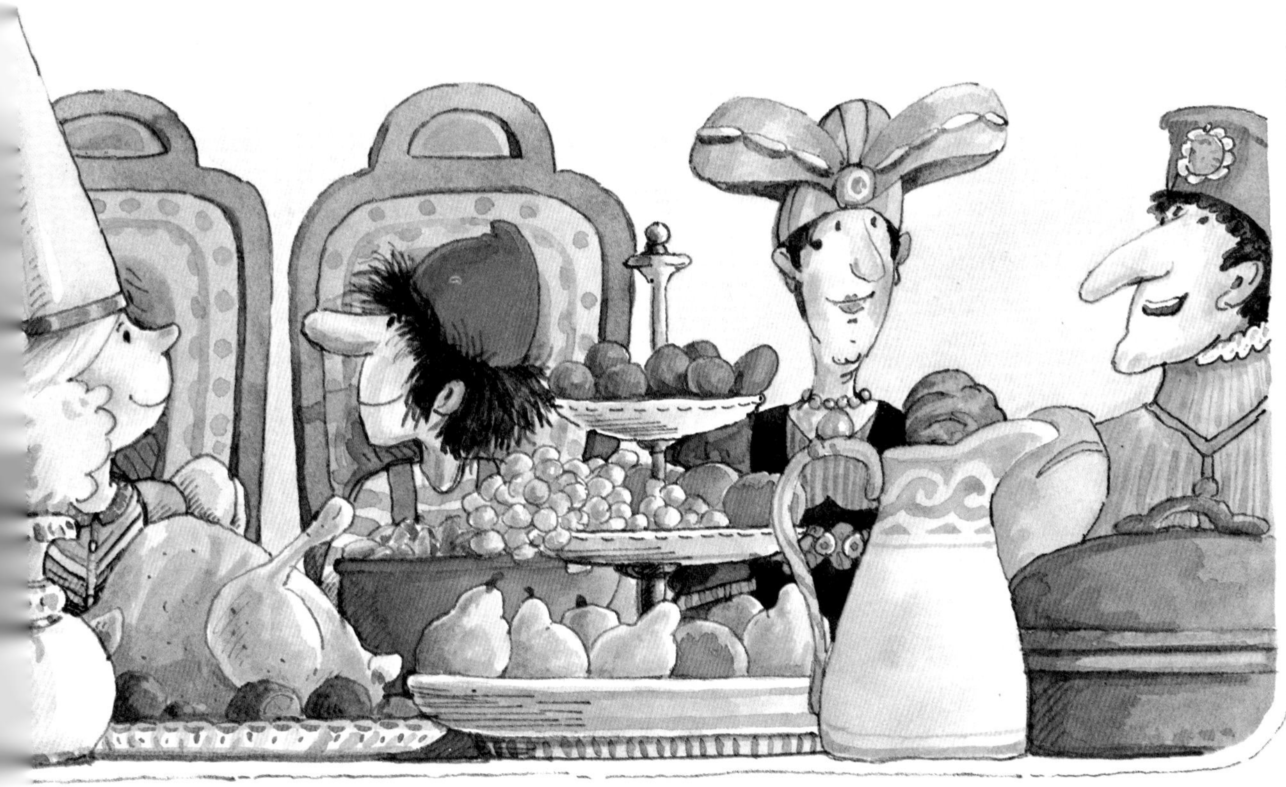

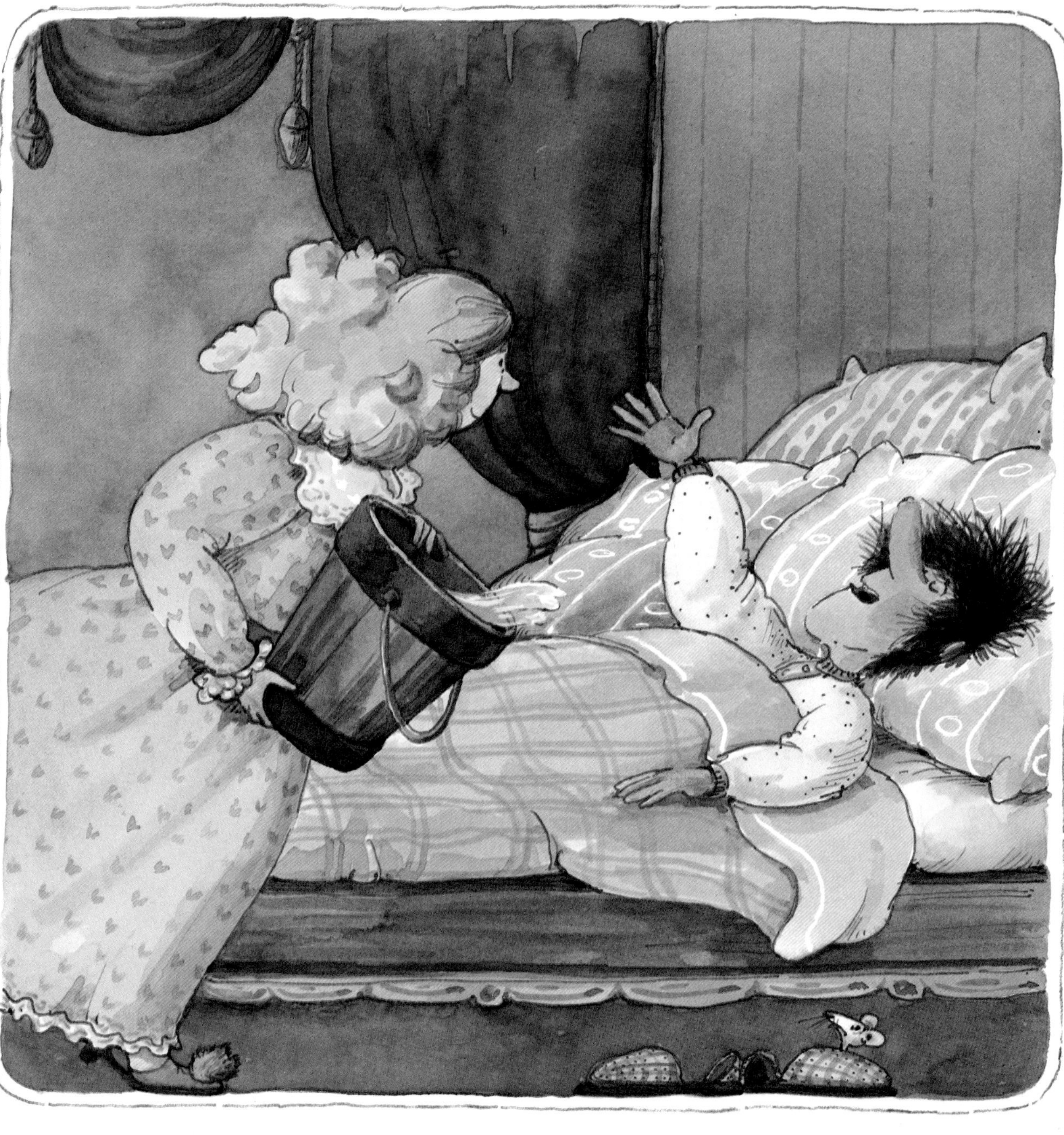

John still wondered about fear often. He even thought about it in his sleep. One night, he talked in his sleep so loudly that he woke the princess.

"Fear, fear! What is fear? Will I never know?" he said.

Now the princess wanted to make her husband happy, so she decided to show him fear. She tiptoed out of the room and fetched a pail of ice-cold water. She threw the water over John's face. *Splash!*

"Aaaagh!" he screamed as he leaped out of bed. He trembled with fear all the way down to his toes. "What happened? What was that?"

"That was fear," laughed the princess. "You were frightened half to death!"

"Aaah! So I was!" said John, and he gave the princess a hug. "Now I know what fear is!" he said.

From that day on, he was still a brave man. But he never again ran into danger without first thinking it over. Carefully!